KT-496-655

Farshore

First published in Great Britain 2021 by Farshore

An imprint of HarperCollins*Publishers*
1 London Bridge Street, London SE1 9GF
www.farshore.co.uk

HarperCollins*Publishers*
1st Floor, Watermarque Building, Ringsend Road
Dublin 4, Ireland

Written by Katrina Pallant
Designed by Jessica Coomber
Illustrated by Robin Davies
Map illustration by Dan Crisp

HiT entertainment   CREATED BY BRITT ALLCROFT

Based on the Railway Series by The Reverend W Awdry.
©2021 Gullane (Thomas) Limited.
Thomas the Tank Engine & Friends™ and Thomas & Friends™ are trademarks of Gullane
(Thomas) Limited. ©2021 HIT Entertainment Limited. HIT and the HIT logo are trademarks of
HIT Entertainment Limited.

ISBN 978 0 7555 0112 0
Printed in Italy
1

A CIP catalogue record for this title is available from the British Library.

All rights reserved. No part of this publication may be reproduced,
stored in a retrieval system, or transmitted, in any form or by any means,
electronic, mechanical, photocopying, recording or otherwise, without
the prior permission of the publisher and copyright owner.

Stay safe online. Farshore is not responsible for content hosted by third parties.

Farshore takes its responsibility to the planet and its inhabitants very seriously.
We aim to use papers from well-managed forests run by responsible suppliers.

MIX
Paper from
responsible sources
FSC® C007454

FSC ™ is a non-profit international organisation established to promote
the responsible management of the world's forests. Products carrying the
FSC label are independently certified to assure consumers that they come
from forests that are managed to meet the social, economic and
ecological needs of present and future generations,
and other controlled sources.

Find out more about HarperCollins and the environment at
www.harpercollins.co.uk/green

London Borough of Tower Hamlets

9100000 8123084

This book
belongs to

AFIF

AFIF

AFIF

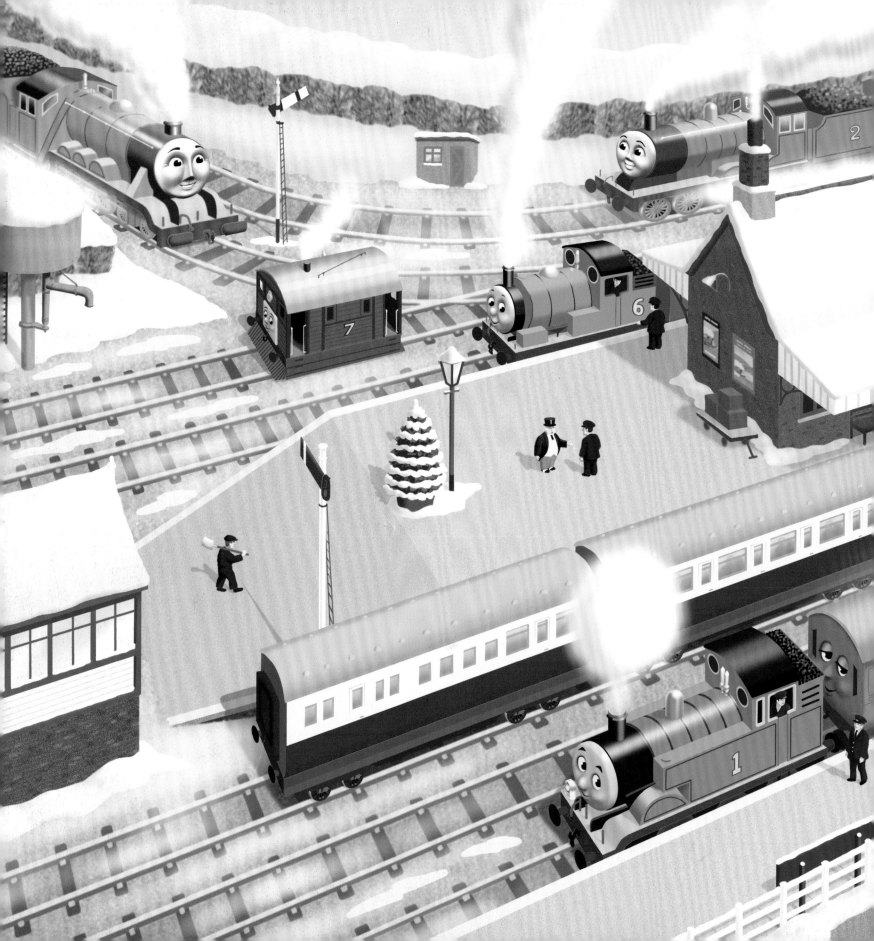

Thomas Saves Christmas

This is a story about Thomas, the Really Useful Engine, and how he had to work together with his friends to deliver some presents …

It was **Christmas Eve** on Sodor and the tracks were covered with snow. Thomas and Percy were ready to do their final jobs in time for Christmas Day.

"Oh, Thomas!" Percy said. "The children in the village will be **so excited** to receive their presents."

"Yes," smiled Thomas. "We must finish clearing the snow off the track so Henry's deliveries don't get delayed!"

Thomas and Percy **rushed** back and forth clearing the snow so Henry could deliver the presents to the villagers.

Percy moved the trucks out of the way.

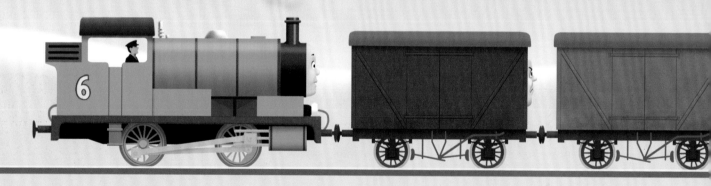

Puff! Puff!

Push! Push!

And Thomas took the last passengers home for the holidays.

Thomas and Percy were tired but happy when all their jobs were done. But The Fat Controller didn't look happy at all.

"I'm afraid to say Henry has not been able to deliver the presents to the village," he said.

"Oh no!" thought Thomas. "Perhaps we didn't clear the snow properly."

"Every time Henry has tried to get to the village he has been **blocked** by mysterious accidents!" The Fat Controller continued.

Henry had set off that morning with his trucks laden with presents, but soon found his way was blocked. Something had caused James to **wobble** and his cargo of logs had rolled across the track.

When the logs were cleared away and Henry could carry on his journey, he **crashed** straight into trucks that Edward had left on the wrong line.

Henry had to return to the Steamworks to be repaired.

"This is terrible. Who is going to deliver the presents now?" said The Fat Controller.

"Don't worry, sir!" Thomas said. "We'll deliver the presents!"

"We won't let those children down!" cried Percy.

Thomas and Percy were worried. It must have been the snow causing so many problems and it had been their job to clear the tracks. But the snow kept falling deeper and deeper!

"Don't worry, you two," Oliver said as he pulled up beside them. "It isn't the snow on the tracks causing all the trouble, it's Father Christmas!"

"What do you mean?" asked Thomas. "How can Father Christmas make everyone have accidents?"

"James and Edward told me they spotted him in the sky. They both got distracted and made mistakes."

Thomas and Percy were excited to hear that they might be able to see **Father Christmas!**

"Remember Percy, we have **to be careful.** We don't want to have accidents like the other engines," Thomas told him.

The pair rolled slowly through Sodor working again to clear the snow. Then **all of a sudden**, a large shadow appeared in the sky.

"It's Father Christmas!" Percy said excitedly.

"No," Thomas said. "That's just Harold. It must have been him all along!"

Thomas and Percy laughed. But Harold did not look happy.

"Thomas, Percy, I'm glad I've found you!" he said. "Snow has blocked every road and track into the village."

"Oh no!" Percy cried. "What about the presents?"

"Don't worry, I know what to do!" Thomas said.

Thomas and Percy rushed to collect Terence the Tractor, who could help them **clear the snow.**

The engines cleared the lower tracks and Terence cleared the nearby roads.

Then Terence was loaded up behind Thomas and Percy **buffered** up behind him, so they could head up the mountain track to the village.

Getting Terence up the mountain was hard work. Thomas and Percy had to go very **slowly**. When they tried to go faster, their wheels slipped and spun on the icy rails. But they kept going together.

Then at last, they saw the village. They were very tired, but they huffed their hardest, until they were safely in the station.

Terence then **whizzed** around the village roads, clearing away the last of the snow. Just then, Percy heard a **buzzing** noise in the sky. It was Harold again! He was dropping parcels of food for the villagers and their pets.

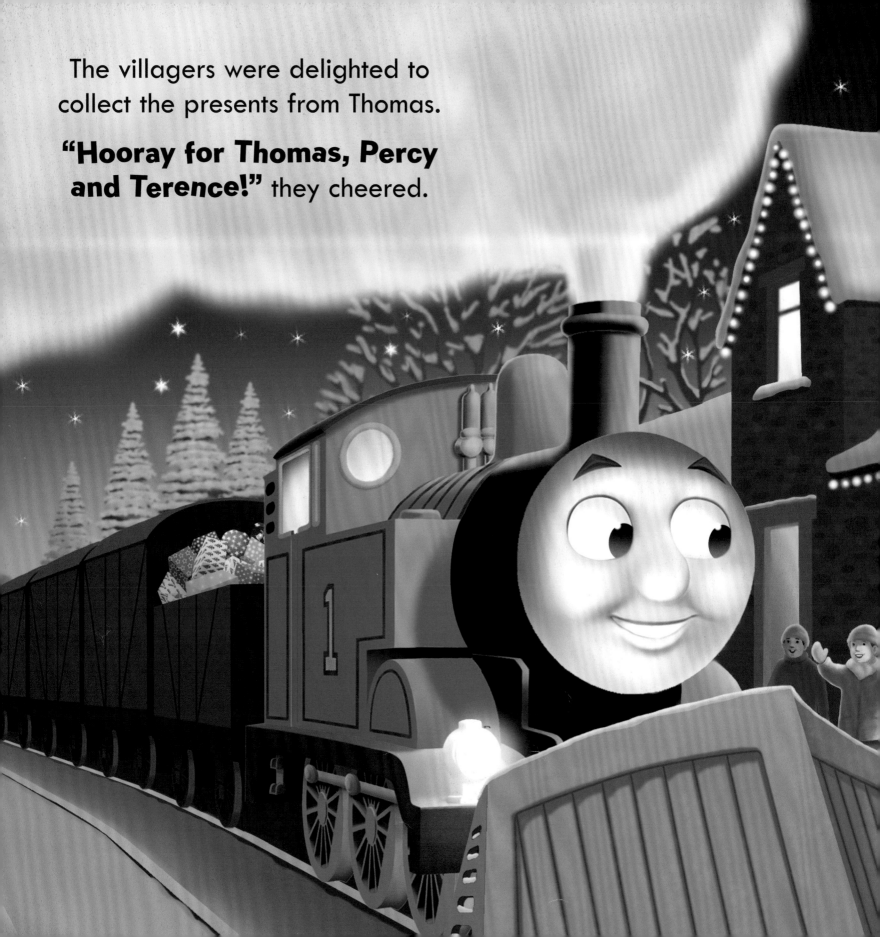

The villagers were delighted to collect the presents from Thomas.

"Hooray for Thomas, Percy and Terence!" they cheered.

Later, as Thomas headed back to Tidmouth Sheds, he was pleased that Christmas had been saved. He peeped goodnight to Harold, chuckling about how he had been mistaken for Father Christmas.

"But wait," he thought. **"If Harold's here, what's that in the sky?"**

He smiled, as he wondered if he had got to see Father Christmas after all!

About the author

The Reverend W. Awdry was the creator of 26 little books about Thomas and his famous engine friends, the first being published in 1945. The stories came about when the Reverend's two-year-old son Christopher was ill in bed with the measles. Awdry invented stories to amuse him, which Christopher then asked to hear time and time again. And now for 75 years, children all around the world have been asking to hear these stories about Thomas, Edward, Gordon, James and the many other Really Useful Engines.

The Reverend Awdry with some of his readers at a model railway exhibition.

The Three Railway Engines, first published in 1945.